Lee Aucoin, *Creative Director*
Jamey Acosta, *Senior Editor*
Heidi Fiedler, *Editor*
Produced and designed by
Denise Ryan & Associates
Illustration © Patrizia Donera
Rachelle Cracchiolo, *Publisher*

Teacher Created Materials

5301 Oceanus Drive
Huntington Beach, CA 92649-1030
http://www.tcmpub.com
Paperback: ISBN: 978-1-4333-5523-3
Library Binding: ISBN: 978-1-4807-1691-9
© 2014 Teacher Created Materials
Printed in China
WaiMan

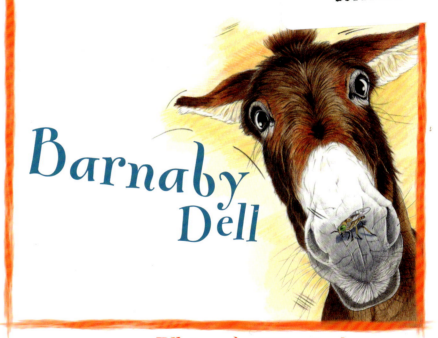

Barnaby Dell

Written by Helen Bethune

Illustrated by Patrizia Donaera

Most farmers are very busy people.
But not Barnaby Dell! He was
the laziest farmer ever.

3

When it was hot, Barnaby took all day to do his chores. The eggs stayed in the henhouse until the next day, and the animals were fed late.

One day, it was very hot. Barnaby milked
the cows. That made him tired.

7

Barnaby sank down in his rocking chair on
the porch. He put his feet on the railing.
Soon, he was fast asleep.

The cat and the dog saw Barnaby sleeping. They decided to have a nap, too. The cows rested under a shady tree.

12

The rooster dozed near the henhouse.
The goat snored gently in the barn. And the
donkey snoozed against the barn wall.
Everything was peaceful.

Suddenly, a nasty horsefly flew over the farm. She was looking for something to bite! She saw the donkey.

ZOOM!

She flew down. She bit the donkey hard on the nose.

"HEE-HAW!" he brayed. He kicked and kicked. He kicked so hard that the goat in the barn woke with a start. She ran into the henhouse.

"COCK-A-DOODLE-DOO," crowed the rooster. He woke the cows.

"MOO!" the cows moaned. One stepped on the dog's tail.

"WOOF!" yelped the dog. He scared the cat.

"MEOWWW!" she yowled. She chased the dog into the henhouse. The goat, the rooster, the cat, and the dog ran around the henhouse. They knocked over the hens' boxes. They broke all the eggs.

The hens CACKLED loudly.

19

Barnaby Dell could not sleep through this racket. He stood up. He gazed at all his animals racing around madly.

"Humph," he grunted. "This won't do. How's a man meant to sleep? ENOUGH!" he bellowed.

The animals stopped and looked at Barnaby. And that was that. Barnaby settled back into his chair on the porch. The animals went back to sleep. All was still again.

But just above the farm, the horsefly hovered . . .
waiting.